AF480616
This book belongs to:

RICHARD'S CHANGING TREE

Charma-Lee Ritchie

Illustrated by Lisa Davis

ISBN # 979-881-88599-9-6

Edited, Designed & Illustrated by Lisa Davis
 - thecraftppl@gmail.com

This book was created for all children,
especially for my son,
Richard Bailey.
With love from,
Mommy and Daddy.

Never forget that you are loved enormously.

Cheers to all moms and dads!
We have the best job in the world!

I have a sugar maple tree.
My dad planted it just for me.

Although I'm growing taller,
my tree is taller than me.

I like to give it water
each morning and
each night, for I want
it to be healthy and
to grow just right.

Its leaves are
broad and green
and gives me
lots of shade,
especially in the
summer when the
sun burns
like a
flame.

I get so hot from playing,
running and tumbling with glee
that my body drips so much water.

"That's PERSPIRATION",
mom says to me.

She says to stay hydrated
and keep my body cool;
we must drink lots of water.
It is brain fuel.

Oh how I love the summer.
The days are long and fun.
But something strange is happening now:
the leaves are yellow, each one!

The days are shorter and cooler.
Nights come quickly, I see.
My mom says this is autumn,
but what will happen to my tree?

Its leaves are
all falling.
I tried putting
them back on
the tree, but mom
laughed, and
dad raked.

Then mom said,
"Come jump in the leaves
with me!"

The leaves are
brown and dry,
but jumping is
so much fun.
The dried leaves
will become plant
food and help our
environment
a ton.

Mom says it is a chemical reaction
that makes the green leaves change.
Each leaf produces chlorophyll.
Yes, that word is strange.
Chlorophyll is a pigment that makes all
leaves look green , but when the season
turns to autumn, new colors can be seen.

One day I will understand
all the things that cause this change,
but for now I will enjoy
the beautiful color range.

Before long the leaves are all gone.
My tree looks oh so sad.
It only has brittle branches.
Maybe my scarf will make it glad.

I do not enjoy the winter much
as it is too cold to play.
But soon winter will be over,
and the snow will go away.

There are a few things about winter
that bring me so much joy;
like making snow angels with mommy,
and receiving a brand new toy.

I also enjoy the
cookies and being
with my family.
Everyone is so happy
except for my cold
little tree.

mom

Mom says spring is coming and my tree will be happier when it gets new green leaves and the birds come out again.

The animals will come out to play after hiding from the cold. The birds will sing their joyful songs until the day is old.

Spring is finally here!
Rabbits and squirrels pop up.
Butterflies dance merrily,
and the flowers bloom a lot.

The days are
warm and bright.
The sky is blue and clear.
Sometimes there is a
sprinkle of rain here
and there.

The air smells fresh and clean
as I fill up my lungs.

I can run, tumble,
and play now
until the day is done.

Oh how I love the seasons.
My favorites are summer and spring,
when my tree is always happy
and the real fun can begin.

Word Find Fun
AIR
AUTUMN
BIRDS
BUNNY
BUTTERFLIES
CHLOROPHYLL
FLOWERS
HYDRATE
LEAF
LUNGS
PERSPIRE
RAIN
SCARF
SKY
SPRING
SUMMER
SUNSHINE
SQUIRREL
TREE
WATER
WINTER

A I R O R T S U M M E R X Z
Y H J C C F L O W E R S T A
H U V L U N G S J W C B L U
Y P O E X S Z R P I H B M T
D F B A E Q I Y E N L U N U
R A I F K U R W R T O N S M
A Q R P L I H U S E R N U N
T Z D Q T R E E P R O Y N E
E P S L A R N T I S P R S S
T R W A T E R E R C H A H K
P O D A L Y F E A Y I I Y
S P R I N G R Y O R L N N R
H E A B U T T E R F L I E S